A LOVE LETTER TO ME

CREATING CONSCIOUS

AWARENESS THROUGH

AFFIRMATIONS

DR. CALENTHIA YVETTE MILLER

A'Lure Publishing LLC

By Dr. Calenthia Miller

For information contact:
www.alurepublishingllc.com
www.Facebook.com/calenthiayvettemiller
www.info@alurepublishingllc.com
www.Facebook.com/alurepublishingllc
@calenthiamiller
@alurepublishing
www.canvasofthought.shop

DEDICATION

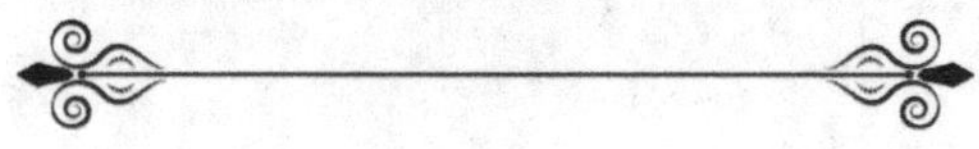

This book is a tribute to anyone who strives to discover and fulfill their unique purpose in life.

AFFIRMATION

noun

emotional support or encouragement

Contents

ACKNOWLEDGMENTS

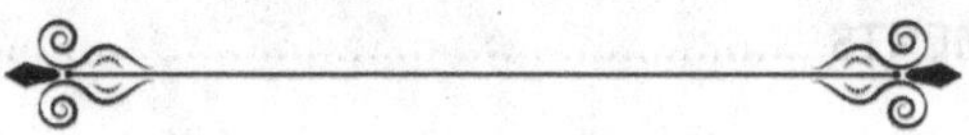

I give honor to God for guiding me and fulfilling His purpose and plan for my life.

I also want to thank my children, Lorenzo and Kahari, for their unwavering support as I continue to carry out this work. To my beautiful granddaughter, Armoni, thank you for simply being yourself.

A special thanks to my work family at Sage Road Pediatrics for being there in my time of need. If not for your quick thinking, my story could have been different.

Lastly, thank you to my bestie, Elogeia 'Mikki "Hadley, for referring me to S.H.E. Publishing, LLC, where I met the owner, Shenitha Finesse, who believed in me and my writing. I am forever grateful for the continuous support, partnership, and sisterhood we have formed in such a short period.

PROLOGUE

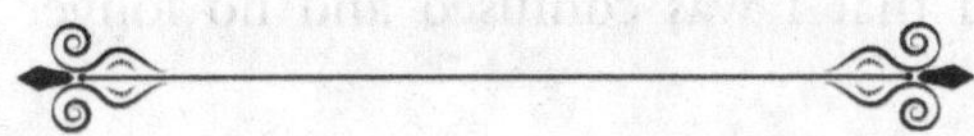

It was just a regular day, like any other. The sun had risen, and I began my morning routine. I woke up at 6:15 a.m., said my prayers, and prepared for work. Around 8:00 a.m., I left my home and headed towards my workplace. After a thirty-minute drive, I finally arrived.

My colleagues greeted me as I walked in, and as usual, I greeted them back with a smile. I went to my office and placed my belongings on my desk. Soon after, I joined my team at the meeting spot, where we usually chat and joke around. Everything seemed normal, with no signs of any unusual occurrences.

It was noon, and I was back in my office when one of my colleagues came in and told me, "You look tired; you need to take some time off." I responded jokingly, "I'm alright," while holding two Aleve pills and a bottle of water in my hand.

Suddenly, I began to feel a headache followed by nausea. I waited for a few minutes, and the symptoms subsided.

However, after two hours, I felt sick again. This time, the symptoms were intense, and I had nausea, vomiting, dizziness, blurred vision, and an unbearable headache that required me to lay my head on the desk. I told one of my colleagues that I was not feeling well and had to leave for home. By then, several other colleagues had come into my office to check on me, and they noticed that I was confused and no longer responding verbally.

My colleagues immediately sprang into action. They called EMS and my family. Within a few minutes, I was transported to the hospital. Once there, my family was told I had a stroke, and if it was not for my work family, my story could have been different.

I spent the next few days in the Neurological ICU, followed by rehab for five months. I fell into a deep depression and did not see a way out. My independence had been taken away. I could not perform tasks we take for granted, like walking, talking, eating, or bathing. It was only by His grace that I am here.

As someone in healthcare for over thirty-five years, I will be the first to say and admit that I did not heed my body's warnings. I have high blood pressure, pre-diabetes, and a cardiac family history. I knew better and did not act better. I had been working under stress for so long that it became my norm. The signs were there, but I chose to ignore them.

This has been such a humbling experience and has taught me

a lot. The first lesson is never to take anything for granted, like your family and health. Learning to manage up and let go is essential in personal care. I still have residual effects of the stroke, which sometimes can be challenging. However, they are manageable and remind me to put me first. Loving yourself is the best gift that you can give yourself.

As we navigate through the complexities of life, we are bound to encounter obstacles that may seem insurmountable. We may find ourselves unsure and lost despite believing in our capacity to overcome even the most trivial challenges. We may feel confined, with no clear path for escaping our predicament. However, we must remember that we can always find a way forward with resilience and determination.

This is my journey of healing and rediscovering who I am. And how daily personal written affirmations and inspirational quotes have shown me how to value my self-worth and reclaim my identity.

DISCLAIMER: I am not a licensed therapist. These are accounts of events in my life.

Pick your battles; it can save your life.

INTRODUCTION

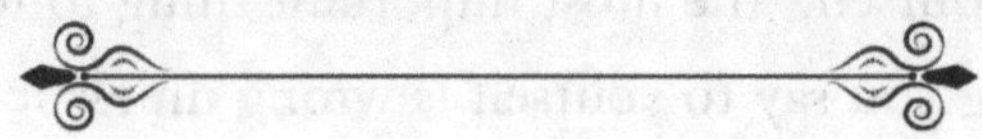

What does it mean to love yourself?

Loving oneself is an essential yet complex concept that encompasses different things. It goes beyond just taking time to care for oneself. It involves taking proactive steps to promote inner peace, such as practicing meditation, engaging in healthy activities, and promoting a me moment by treating oneself to things like a facial or massage.

Furthermore, it could also mean indulging in a luxurious staycation at a nice hotel, allowing yourself to be pampered and cared for, even if only for a short time.

Loving oneself affirms your worthiness to receive love, care, support, and adoration. It means recognizing that you deserve these things because you should not settle for less.

It is essential to understand that our words have value in our lives and others. Therefore, committing to loving ourselves unconditionally, without any boundaries, is crucial. Doing so can create a positive and healthy relationship with yourself, ultimately leading to a better quality of life.

Dr. Calenthia, how do I accomplish this?

Writing a love letter to yourself can be a powerful exercise to motivate, encourage, and uplift yourself to become the best version of yourself. The most important thing to remember is that nothing you say to yourself is wrong unless it is negative. Therefore, it is crucial to be mindful when choosing your words. The result of writing a love letter to yourself is that you will feel good about yourself. Moreover, those around you will see the positive light that illuminates each time they are in your presence. Allowing yourself to be authentic and not pretending to be something you are not will give you the freedom to evolve into the person you are meant to be.

Dr. Maya Angelou best said it.

"I've learned that people will forget what you said, people will forget what you did, but people will never forget how you made them feel."

"Setbacks are not failures. They are opportunities for us to reevaluate our assignments."

LOVE LETTER

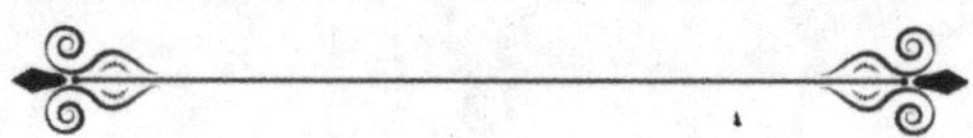

My love letter to me started two weeks after I had my stroke. I had just returned from one of my therapy sessions. I remember sitting at the edge of the bed in tears. My body hurt, and I could not see myself living like this. Every day in pain, I could not do anything for myself. My sons helped me do everything from bathing, putting on my clothes, and eating. This was not the life I wanted and, indeed, not what I envisioned for my boys. I did not want to be a burden.

I heard this robust voice fill the room and echo in my ear. ' What can you not do?"

I knew immediately that it was God speaking to me.

Let me give this disclaimer: I don't push religion off on anyone. But I know a higher power was in that hospital room when I flatlined again in my bedroom that day.

God repeated, "What can you not do?"

"I said I cannot live like this."

God replied, "Do you think I want you to suffer?"

I said," No."

God said, "Sometimes we must go through the fire, but that doesn't mean you will be burned. So, tell me again, what you cannot do?"

I was silent for a moment. I began to think, why not me?

God continued, "I planted a seed in you, and now it is time for you to water them."

I replayed back all of the events that had transpired before the stroke. I remember God saying to me. "Be quiet, stay still, and listen."

 In August 2021, I lost my ability to speak for two months. I went to several doctors, including an ENT, who specialist in disorders of your ears, nose, and throat. The doctor performed a laryngoscopy, a test that visualized the larynx, "the voice box" revealed nothing. The doctor could not explain why I was not able to speak. About two weeks later, I had a bilateral ear infection and a severe upper respiratory infection. I had to go through several weeks of voice therapy and antibiotics. But remember, God told me, "Be quiet, stay still and listen." This was His way of getting my attention. I was still not obedient, which brought me to January 19, 2022, and ultimately, to this love letter to me.

February 2, 2022, at 9:54 AM- A Journal Just for Me.
Good morning, Queen,

I am truly grateful to see another beautiful day, as so many were not on that call list. I don't take it for granted the opportunity to listen to Him who has created me.

The one who has shown favor, the one who has gone to battle for me, the one who has stepped in the gap for me, the one who soothes the pain and wipes away the tears from my eyes, the one who listens without judgment. It is He that I serve and step out on faith for, knowing He will be there to support me with love and yet allow me to fall but not fail.

Reflecting on the events of January 20-25, I realize that my purpose is to give back, for He has given me this platform to pay it forward. He has given me the knowledge that needs to be heard by others. Step out on faith, be bold, and spread your wings and fly. The most extraordinary ideas are buried in the cemetery. You are not dead; you are among the living.

Today, I affirm I will be heard and no longer trapped by my past. I am looking forward to new opportunities and blessings. No longer scared of the unknown. Be bold, beautiful, and brave.

Doc Diva

After writing this letter the next day, God said, "*What do you like to do?*"

My reply was, "I like to write."

God responded, "*I know you do, so what are you waiting on.*"

God gave me the words to write my first book, **UNMASK**, in four weeks and my second book, **UNMASK 2- Uncovering the Truth**, in six weeks. Both were published and released in less than a year. And have been purchased overseas within a week of their release dates. God continues to direct me as I stand in my purpose to do this fantastic work.

The words you speak and hear profoundly impact your development and how you view yourself. Positive verbal affirmation and self-preservation can be a life changer. You are your advocate. Be proactive in your happiness.

Critical things to remember are:
- Get to know yourself.
- Be kind to yourself.
- Practice saying" NO"
- Stop comparing yourself to others.
- Reward yourself just because.
- Finding the good within yourself.
- Doing what you love

A positive self-image is a foundation for greater confidence in developing a higher sense of self-worth. I also suggest working with a good, licensed therapist. A therapist is your advocate who provides a safe, judgment-free environment. It's okay not to be okay.

"Life lessons are crucial milestones in the development of our personal growth. Surround yourself with people willing to hold you accountable for your actions. And certainly, be there to celebrate your accomplishments."

THE JOURNEY

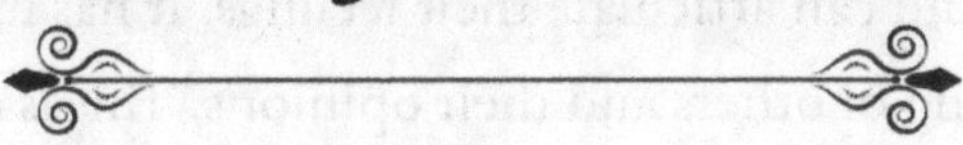

Any achievement's true worth or value can only be measured by the people actively working towards it. This is because they are the ones who understand the amount of effort, dedication, and persistence required to reach the goal. Their experiences and challenges faced during the journey provide a unique perspective that outsiders may not fully comprehend. Therefore, when evaluating the merits of an achievement, it's crucial to consider the perspective of those who have put in the work to attain it.

I began my journey of journaling when I was about eight years old and writing poetry and short stories at the age of nine. Journaling allowed me to record and unpack my thoughts and feelings on paper. But it also allowed me to escape into a world my vivid and vibrant mind created. A world that took me to places I never imagined I would go. Then life happened, and journaling was replaced with being an adult with responsibilities. After my stroke, I returned to journaling and writing to enhance my cognitive skills, reduce stress, and help me focus on a balanced lifestyle. It also clarified many things that had been unclear for many years.

My journaling has since evolved into creative writing and posting affirmations and inspirational quotes on my social media platforms. In posting, I found that more people are more open and can articulate their feelings. It has improved my understanding of others and their opinions. This is also my way of being obedient, paying it forward, and spreading positivity and social awareness to the masses.

In this journey, you must do self-checks and inventory. It is crucial to allow yourself grace when you can't tolerate unnecessary chaos and confusion. This might mean you must reconsider those who no longer serve a purpose in this season of your life. It doesn't mean you don't care for them. It simply means that you have outgrown one another. This happens in so many relationships. Self-preservation is critical to survival.

Survival Guide to Self-Preservation
- Set boundaries!
- Prioritizing free time versus available time
- Allocate downtime to relax and regroup.
- Nourish your mind, body, and spirit.
- Love you.
- Again, set boundaries. Cut off that which may harm you.

A LOVE LETTER TO ME

Although change can be a daunting experience, it is essential to acknowledge its significance and welcome it with open arms. Remaining static and unchanging can lead to a lack of growth and progress. Start practicing the act of self-love; it will give you unspeakable joy.

"Great accomplishment comes with fear. You control
whether you are willing to rebuke or reject it."

AFFIRMATIONS

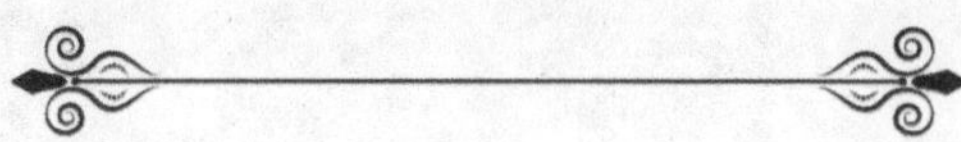

Daily affirmation should be said as it is happening now. When speaking it to be so, you have affirmed that it will come to pass. Now begin your journey of proclaiming it.

"I Am….." Never sell yourself short, as you are your own best investment.

Now It's Your Turn. Read, Reflect, and Respond. The examples are not all affirmations but inspirational quotes as well. Both have garnered exciting conversations on my social media page and podcast Confessions of a Publisher with my co-host Shenitha Finesse.

Instruction

Read the affirmation or inspirational quote entirely. It is okay if you must reread for a second time for clarity. Once you have read, take some time to dissect and reflect on the words and think of a situation or event that may be relevant.

Now, it is time to respond. Remember, no answer is a wrong answer. It is what you think.

Read

"I will never be the obstacle that prevents me from reaching my goal."

Reflect

....
....
....
....
....
....

Response

....
....
....
....
....
....
....

A LOVE LETTER TO ME

Read

"I am like no other. Victorious."

Reflect

....
....
....
....
....
....
....

Response

....
....
....
....
....
....
....

Read

"The winning circle is not always about the person within it but those outside it who have worked just as hard to get them there."

Reflect

....
....
....
....
....
....
....

Response

....
....
....
....
....
....
....

Read

"Understanding of others is our ability to no longer operate out of fear and ignorance."

Reflect

....
....
....
....
....
....
....

Response

....
....
....
....
....
....
....

Read

"Being humble is your way of understanding that you don't have the answer to everything. And guess what, that's OK!"

Reflect

....
....
....
....
....
....
....

Response

....
....
....
....
....
....
....

Read.

"I see the infinite possibilities within me. So, I will, I must, and I can."

Reflect

....

....

....

....

....

....

....

Response

....

....

....

....

....

....

....

Now that you have come to the end of the exercise. It is time to seize the moment. The finish line is in sight. What are you waiting for? There is no turning back now. You have done the hard work. The seed has now been planted. It is now up to you to water it. Continue to take the time to affirm and celebrate you!

Your Love Letter

....
....
....
....
....
....
....
....
....
....
....
....
....
....
....
....
....
....
....
....
....
....

Affirmation or Inspirational Quote

Read

....
....
....
....
....
....
....

Reflect

....
....
....
....
....
....
....

Response

....
....
....
....
....

Read

Reflect

Response

CLOSING REMARKS

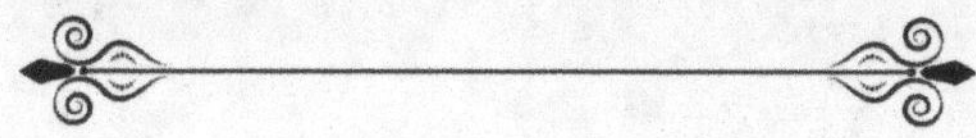

It has taken many years for me to get to the place where I can look in the mirror and say, "I am enough and love the woman I am and become. Never allow your enemies to devalue who you are and the path in which you are traveling. Remember, self-doubt is like a weed until you unroot it. Be bold and brave as you affirm who you are and your existence in this world. In closing, I would like to thank you for your support in purchasing my book. I hope the words within these pages will guide those who long to find direction and meaning in their lives.

Dr. Calenthia Miller

"Your legacy should not be determined by the amount of money you make. But by the amount of people you have invested in by empowering, encouraging, and elevating to the next level."

REFLECTIONS

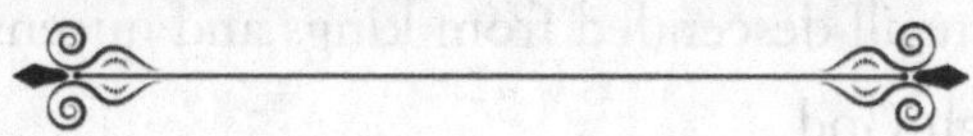

Spoken Word July 2023 Family Reunion

As I sat down to write these words in my journal. I began to reflect on this remarkable journey that I have endured. Please let me clarify that we all have a story to tell. And my story is unique like yours is to you.

We all have cried in the midnight hours, experienced sleepless nights, and bore many battle scars seen and unseen. But, through it all, we made it by the grace of God. We weathered the storm and have made it to this day.

A day of reflection of stories untold. It is a story that bridges the bloodlines of our ancestors whose shoulders we stand upon— the men and women who have faced unimaginable hardships, struggles, and death for being simply black.

As you take this time to peer in the eyes of those kin folk next to you and gaze upon the melanin that tints their skin, this is the physical byproduct of our DNA. A molecular fiber that connects us all.

Our bloodline is a piece of our history. A history that reminds us that we are all descended from kings and queens created by the most high God.

Remember that the choices that we make today leave an impression on the generation that is coming behind us.

So, walk with the boldness that we are all made of. We no longer prescribe to the narrative that we are less than as we know we are more than enough.

As we all leave this place and return to our homes, please take the time to honor those who have paved the way for us all. A path of generational wealth, knowledge, and love that binds us all.

In conclusion, this journey begins with those closest to you - your family. Plant the seeds that allow us all to reap the harvest.

Dr. Calenthia Miller

COMING SOON FROM
DR. CALENTHIA MILLER

UNMASK BOOK 3-TAKING THE NEXT STEP

UNMASK BOOK 4-WORTH FIGHTING FOR

Creative Conversation with Dr. C.- Inaugural Podcast January of 2024 via Facebook Live and YOUTUBE.